Call Me Penny Pickleberry

A STORY *to* HELP KIDS MANAGE WORRIES

MEGHAN GRANA

Illustrated by Fanny Liem

BIRD
UPSTAIRS

AUTHOR'S NOTE

For many children, anxiety can present a huge obstacle to engaging in everyday activities. As caregivers, we can support children by teaching them how to recognize what anxiety feels like, how to question negative thoughts for validity, and how to persevere even when we feel unsure. *Call Me Penny Pickleberry* provides families with an opportunity to discuss fears or worries and learn strategies to overcome them. And I hope it brings a bit of fun to your day as well.

For Georgia and Josephine, may you always listen to your Pennys. And for my personal barista, PJ, who responds to every one of my wild ideas with, "You should totally do that." —MG

Published by Bird Upstairs Books™, Seattle
www.birdupstairs.com

Produced by Girl Friday Productions

Design: Paul Barrett
Development & editorial: Kristin Duran
Production editorial: Bethany Davis

ISBN (hardcover): 978-1-954854-58-1
ISBN (e-book): 978-1-954854-59-8

Library of Congress Control Number: 2022900363

First edition

Meet Penelope Pickleberry, first grader extraordinaire, ringleader of success, architect of her own bright future! She can tie her shoelaces in under thirty seconds, pack her own mom-approved snack bag, and build an entire mouse hotel out of milk cartons. Penelope Pickleberry is simply spectacular!

But Penelope has one HUGE problem . . .

Nelly!

Nelly is the voice in Penelope's head that tells her about bad things that might happen, like getting chased by a swarm of bees or finding a shark in the swimming pool.

Sometimes, Nelly reminds Penelope about her most embarrassing moments, like when she burped during the Pledge of Allegiance or got the stub of a movie ticket stuck up her nose.

And other times, Nelly tries to scare
Penelope into avoiding something new, like
trying a fun sport or making a new friend
or eating a chocolate-covered grasshopper.

Nelly is a total pest.

Luckily, Penelope has Penny to listen to, the smarter voice in her head. Penny has truth-telling superpowers. She reminds Penelope that she CAN ride a two-wheeled bike, be a fantastic class messenger, and even learn how to use chopsticks. Penny believes Penelope can do almost anything!

Penny and Nelly spend much of their time disagreeing.
At recess, they both have a lot to say.

"You'll never get across those
monkey bars," Nelly says. "When
you fall right on your bottom, ALL
the kids will laugh and call you
Penelope Pickle*bottom*!"

"SHUSH!" says Penny. "Just try to get across the first three bars, Penelope. Each day it will get easier, and soon you'll make it across like a ninja warrior!"

But Nelly sounds so convincing that Penelope starts to believe her. Soon her arms feel wobbly. When Penelope tries to swing across the bars, she only barely makes it to the third rung.

Penny and Nelly will not keep quiet during math class either.

"Time for Math Centers!" the teacher says. "Kids, partner up and grab a pair of dice!"

"No one wants to be YOUR partner," Nelly tells Penelope. "You never know whether you're supposed to add or subtract. And I bet you'll get the dice that Henry Higgleworm put under his armpit yesterday."

"Don't listen to her," Penny responds. "Nobody gets the answers right ALL the time. Not even Vivian, and she won the Mad Math Minute contest last year. Be brave! Try asking someone to be your partner."

Penelope feels frozen and wishes someone would ask her.
But before she can get the courage, all the kids pair up. And
Penelope is left to work alone . . . with
Henry Higgleworm's stinky dice.

When Mom and Dad have a date night, Penny and Nelly go at it again.

Nelly starts up right away. "The babysitter is going to burn the popcorn. Mom and Dad will forget to kiss you good night. What if you can't find Mr. Bunny when it's time for bed? WHO WILL FIND MR. BUNNY?"

But Penny reassures Penelope. "You're going to kiss Mom and Dad good night and give them a long, tight hug. Then maybe the babysitter will make a fort or play a board game with you."

Instead of enjoying her time with the babysitter, Penelope stares out the window, hoping Mom and Dad will come home early.

Tomorrow is the final game of the soccer season, and it is against the Purple Pandas. At bedtime, Nelly's voice gets louder. It is hard for Penelope to fall asleep.

"You might oversleep," Nelly warns. "Where is your Sunshine Warriors jersey? Is it clean? You spilled fruit punch on it after the last game."

Penny has a plan. "You have exactly five minutes to think about tomorrow's game," she says. "Set the timer, hold Mr. Bunny tight, and get all your worries out. Coach is bringing doughnuts for the last game. I bet she brings sprinkled strawberry ones, or my favorite—chocolate glazed!"

Finally, comforted by Penny's words and Mr. Bunny, Penelope drifts off to sleep and dreams of sweet treats.

The morning of the big game
arrives. Penelope gets dressed in her
crisp, bright yellow jersey, gobbles up her dad's
world-famous banana pancakes, and heads to the game.

But once they get to the field, Nelly starts up again.

"You haven't scored a single goal this whole season!" says Nelly. "You're not fast enough. You trip over your own feet. Kids don't pass the ball to you because they know you'll mess up."

But Penny has other ideas.

"Penelope, you're fast and have a strong kick. You're the loudest cheerleader on the sidelines! You are the sunshiniest Warrior there is!" Penny reminds her.

Penelope realizes that each time she listens to Nelly, she ends up feeling sad or disappointed, but Penny makes her feel confident and powerful. Penny is always on her side.

Penelope hits the field like a rocket ship. She sprints, she dribbles, she cheers. She is on top of the world!

Nelly's voice gets softer and quieter until Penelope can hardly hear it anymore.

In the final few moments of the game, the Sunshine Warriors are down two to one. Penelope's teammate Daphne has the ball and runs toward the goal when a Purple Panda blocks her. Her eyes shoot up. There is Penelope, wide open.

Daphne passes the ball.

Penelope takes control of the ball and dribbles it down the field. Right before her eyes—there is a clear shot at goal.

She boots the ball as hard as she can, catapulting it into the air toward the goal. Up and up and up it goes . . .

Ding!

The ball hits the crossbar—and bounces straight back to a Purple Panda.

With only seconds left, the Sunshine Warriors lose the game.

And that's when it starts . . . the inside-out squeezing, whirly feeling in Penelope's belly.

Nelly whips out the bullhorn. "It's all your fault! You lost the game for the team. You are the Worst. Player. Ever!"

But Penny jumps right in. "Breathe in and out," she says calmly. "Long, deep breaths. Inhale, like you are smelling a flower. Then exhale, like you are blowing out candles. See? You are OK. Keep breathing."

Penelope puts one foot in front of the other, guided by Penny's kind and gentle words.

"You are a wonderful teammate. You are important to this team. You gave it your all."

And with each one of Penny's soft whispers, Penelope makes it off the field.

Penelope has been so focused on her fears that at first, she doesn't hear her teammates' cheers.

"Nice kick!"   "Good try!"   "Time for doughnuts!"

And there are her teammates, gathering around a pile of sprinkled strawberry doughnuts.

"Penelope, come join us! We have sprinkled strawberry AND chocolate glazed!"

"Thanks. Chocolate glazed is my favorite.

And from now on, you can call me Penny."

A GUIDE FOR SHUSHING YOUR NELLY

Download this page as a poster at www.meghangrana.com

1 Breathe. Take long, deep breaths. Inhale 1, 2, 3, 4, 5. Exhale 1, 2, 3, 4, 5. Breathing resets your body for calmness and relaxes your mind.

2 Get your worries out. Decide how long you are allowed to worry. Set a timer or play your favorite song three times. When the time's up, start an activity you enjoy. You might race your favorite toy cars or create a make-believe classroom with your stuffed animals.

3 Outnumber Nelly. For every negative thought you have about yourself, think of three things you love about yourself. Are you a good friend or a big helper at school? Do you take good care of your pet? Do you give great hugs?

4 Draw it out. When you are feeling sad or anxious, drawing pictures and writing stories can help make you feel better. Your feelings are important, whether you are feeling sad or happy.

5 Create a gratitude journal. Write or draw the parts of your day that you are thankful for. Did a friend share a snack with you? Did you play your favorite game in PE? Maybe you got to pet a friendly neighborhood dog. Small moments like these can add up to real happiness.

Congratulations! You are on your way to overpowering your Nelly!